JONAH

JAN SIKES

JONAH

BY

JAN SIKES

*J*onah planted both feet firmly on the sturdy wooden dock and scanned the horizon. He could almost make out the outline of the mainland. More than once, he'd attempted to swim it. Meeting failure each time, he had to turn back or die.

Would today be the day the boat would arrive? Brown murky water lapped at the timbers, and a scaled water lizard trolled for a morning snack.

A low guttural growl turned him around. The feral creatures on this island were like none he'd ever encountered – half-animal and half-mythical.

In his years of living, Jonah had learned that every creature, human or animal, had a weakness. He'd discovered theirs out of desperation to survive.

He strode down the dock, stopping to scoop up the silver dagger he'd left lying in the sand, then ran toward the creature screaming, dagger aimed at its heart.

Perhaps it was the glint of the sun off the metal

blade. Or perhaps it was the scream that arose inside his chest and spilled out as he ran toward the fanged creature. Jonah didn't know, but it worked every time, as the animal would turn away and disappear noisily back into the thick, tangled brush.

It now seemed like a lifetime ago that the aging judge had banished him to this godforsaken place. *Had it been the right choice?* He questioned himself every day. Maybe prison wouldn't have been so bad after all.

He scanned the horizon one final time before kneeling to light a fire. If he'd known what lay ahead, he might have chosen differently. But, at the time, anything sounded better than being locked in a cement box, buried deep in the ground. No, that was the one thing Jonah could not survive. Unbidden memories of the suffocating small dark closet at the orphanage, constricted his chest.

Sure, they'd given him the dagger and a few meager supplies when they'd dropped him off. Everything else he had to get on his own. And, it didn't help that thick, tangled stinging nettles, flowers filled with deadly venom, and large birds that swooped down without warning and pecked his head, covered the island.

But the creatures were the worst of all. He'd never forget the first time they'd shown themselves. Fangs that glowed red when they growled, and claws like that of eagles, had sent him clamoring through the brush - despite the pain of the stinging nettles and prickly thorns. Their claws and thick bodies allowed them to easily trample through, leaving him with no option but to flee. Exhausted and unable to run anymore, he turned and prepared to die. Instead, when he brandished his dagger and lunged toward them screaming, the creatures backed down and slunk away.

With welts covering his body from the stinging nettles, and sweat dripping down his face, he'd waded into the murky, muddy water, his pain being lessened by the mud.

Driven to construct some sort of shelter, he gathered branches and brush on the first day. Over the many days that followed, tiny improvements were made to the primitive hut.

He kept track of time with marks on a piece of driftwood. It was now covered with thirty marks - and he was still alive. *But, for how long?*

On day thirty-one, Jonah awoke with a start. Hearing the loud thud, his hand automatically flew to his dagger. Warily, he peeked out of his crude shelter, expecting the worst.

There, a few feet from his hut, lay a burlap package.

With darting eyes, he searched the area for the source from which the package had come. He dashed out, grabbed it and quickly ducked back inside. His heart raced. He hadn't been forgotten.

He tore into the package as eager as a child on Christmas morning. The first item he discovered was a sealed package of dried buffalo jerky. Without looking any farther, he tore into it and groaned aloud as he savored the flavor of the meat. Anything was better than the muddy fish and bugs he'd been forced to eat to stay alive.

Jonah's long dark hair fell across his face as he sat

back on his haunches and explored the remaining contents of his mysterious package. A bar of soap, toothbrush, and hairbrush fell out onto the floor of his hut. He set them aside and continued exploring.

In the bottom of the bag lay two books and a pencil, along with a handwritten note. He unfolded the parchment paper.

There is only one way off this island. You must examine yourself, face your truths and make peace with your demons.

Jonah folded the note and lay it next to the bag. Biting off another piece of jerky, then carefully resealing the package, he opened the first book, "The Four Agreements" by Don Miguel Ruiz.

"Be impeccable with your word," he read aloud. He tossed the book into the far corner of the hut. He didn't need any philosophy BS.

He opened the second book. Finding only blank pages, he tossed it into the corner, as well.

He'd heard the psychological and philosophical jargon his entire life and none of it had helped him survive on the streets. None of it had helped when the leather strap landed repeatedly across his back, and none of it had put food in his belly when he was starving.

No. He'd made his way with his own strength, grit, and determination, and that wasn't about to change now.

Running the brush through his hair, he tied it back, then ducked out of the shelter into the early morning dawn. The most important thing he could do was keep his body strong and ready to fight. After all, it was what he did best. He stretched his taut muscles and began a series of Tai Chi maneuvers. Twirling and kicking, he landed in fighting stance. Yes, this was what worked for him, not religion, not psychobabble, and certainly not philosophy.

A scurrying sound drew his attention toward the hut, and he turned just in time to see a furry rodent dash inside. *The jerky!* He lunged forward and reached the critter at the same time it reached the bag. With a precise throw, his dagger landed in the varmint's neck. He tossed the invader over his shoulder into the murky water and grabbed the jerky. After digging a hole, he buried the dried buffalo, placing both books on top for added security.

There. That should keep it out of harm's way. The mushrooms and edible roots he'd discovered several days ago, combined with the buffalo, would make a delicious stew later.

One thing was clear – he didn't need self-examination. What he needed was sustenance. But most of all, he needed to get back to the mainland, back to living, and back to ruling his kingdom on the backstreets of the city.

He pondered the words on the note. *What was he going to be forced to do?*

Thankful for a cooking pot, Jonah hunched over the small fire and drew in the savory smell. His stomach growled. Stirring the mushrooms and Burdock root to a slow boil, he added torn pieces of the jerky.

Startled by the crackling of leaves, Jonah jumped to his feet, reaching for his ever-present dagger. Scanning the area, he saw nothing. *It must have been an animal.* After all, the judge had been very specific in warning him he would be the only human inhabiting the island.

He sat back on his heels and stirred the boiling stew.

There it was again. That time, there was no mistaking the sound of footsteps. *Was he going mad?*

"Who's there?" he yelled out.

Silence responded.

Jonah jumped to his feet and whirled in a circle, scanning the perimeter. He saw nothing out of place, so returned to his stew. Once he was satisfied that it was thoroughly cooked, he pulled the container from the fire and disappeared into his hut to enjoy the fare.

His nostrils flared and eyes closed as the delectable aroma arose. Within minutes, he devoured the tasty concoction.

Just as he wiped his mouth on the back of his hand, he heard it again. Footsteps approached from the north. Perched on one knee, he held his breath, ready to spring. The footsteps stopped just short of his hut.

He let out a loud war cry and lunged from the hut, dagger drawn. To his surprise, a young boy stood wide-eyed, forcing him to a screeching halt.

Jonah had difficulty finding his voice but managed a weak, "Hello."

The boy simply nodded.

"Who are you? Where did you come from?" Jonah fired the questions. "How did you get here? Are you from the mainland?" Jonah quickly deduced this was no ordinary boy. His eyes glowed with luminescent green light and webbing grew between his long fingers.

The boy turned and ran away.

Jonah gave chase, easily overtaking him and pulling the boy to the ground, face down. He turned him over. "I demand some answers. Did the judge send you?"

The boy shook his head. "I didn't know you were here, mister."

"You've got some explaining to do, kid." Jonah helped him to his feet, practically dragging him back toward his camp. The boy cried out in protest as Jonah kept an iron grip on his arm.

"Ouch! You're hurting me!"

"If I let go, you better not run. I promise I can hurt you more than you can imagine." He loosened his grip but maintained contact with the boy.

Reaching his tiny shelter, Jonah pushed the boy inside, landing him on his back. When he crawled in next to him, suddenly, he couldn't find enough air to fill his lungs.

What was it with this kid? He wasn't normal.

"Okay, boy. I need some answers," he demanded, sucking in a breath between his teeth. "Where did you come from?"

The boy shrugged.

"Come on. You came from somewhere. Now, you tell me, or you'll be sorry."

"I can show you, but you have to promise not to hurt me," the boy replied.

"What's wrong with your eyes and hands?" Jonah prodded.

"I don't know what you're talking about."

"Who are you?" Jonah continued, determined to get the answers he sought.

The visitor lifted his chin. "I am Titus, son of Drake and Jade."

Jonah sat back on his haunches. "That tells me nothing. Are you from the mainland?"

Titus pointed toward the faint outline of the giant city over the horizon. "You mean there?"

Jonah nodded in response.

"No. I came through the caves. I was tired of being alone and the deafening silence was making me insane, so I went exploring and found you."

Puzzled, Jonah drew circles in the dirt floor. Remembering stories he'd heard about beings with special powers, he stared hard at the boy. "Are you an Enchanter?"

"I don't know what that is." Titus shifted and spread his webbed hands in front of him. "Let me show you where I live. It is on the other side of this island."

"Fair enough, but don't try anything funny or it will be the last thing you do," Jonah warned, brandishing the dagger.

They exited the hut with Jonah following closely behind the boy, as he moved effortlessly through the brambles and stinging nettles. The needles appeared to magically part, and move out of the boy's way, but then quickly closed back just in time to sting Jonah's skin.

After a mile, the boy stopped short. "This is as far as I can take you. They won't let you go any farther."

Exasperated, Jonah exploded. "They who?"

Without warning, the boy disappeared through a

slim crevice in a rock. Jonah hurried to follow only to be met by a legion of green, slimy snakes blocking the way. Turning to flee, he found more curled up and ready to strike in every direction.

"Titus! Where are you?" he screamed.

His response came by way of hisses and slithering.

2

*J*onah swung his dagger spinning in circles, faster and faster. Oblivious to the poisonous thorns and brambles around him, he vaulted over the snakes and ran as fast as his legs could carry him, back to the pseudo safety of his makeshift camp.

Breath came in ragged gasps, yet he didn't stop running until he was chest deep in the gray, muddy water that surrounded his prison. He pounded the water with angry fists while releasing a string of curses.

Jonah spent the next two days nursing his wounds and scouring the area where Titus had disappeared. It was as if the earth had swallowed him up and left no traces.

He kept a wary eye out for the snakes that had blocked his path days before, but there was no sign of them having ever been there. *Had he imagined the entire event?* He'd heard stories about men going mad; maybe now he was one of those men.

After another futile search of the area, he sought shelter from the brutal mid-day sun inside his makeshift hut. He hoped Titus would make another appearance. If he did, he wouldn't let him slip away again.

His gaze landed on the discarded books in the corner. Deciding he had nothing better to do with his time, he reached for "The Four Agreements" and opened it.

"To the Circle of Fire; those who have gone before, those who are present and those who have yet to come," the opening page began.

Jonah puzzled over the reference to the Circle of Fire. He remembered a time back on the mainland when he'd hidden in the woods and observed a group of scantily clad women dancing around a fire, uttering chants and incantations. His eyes crinkled at the corners at the memory. The only thought in his head at the time, was undressing the one with the golden hair.

He read on.

Chapter 1: "What you are seeing and hearing right now is nothing but a dream. You are dreaming right now in this moment. You are dreaming with the brain awake..."

A dream? Well, I don't like this dream so I'm going to change it. As was habit, Jonah suckled air between his teeth.

He read farther. Before he knew it, the sun set, and the sky turned a bright red and orange. *How had he lost so many hours reading this book? And, why had he even bothered to read it in the first place?* Most of it was pure common sense. Keeping your word and not taking things personally were tools of the trade he'd learned long ago, living on the streets. Although, if he were to be honest, he'd never placed much value on keeping his word. Making sure others kept their word to him held more importance.

But, one thing the book hadn't covered was fear. Although not his own, it was fear that had kept him alive. He'd earned a vicious reputation over time, and everyone within his path quickly learned to respect and fear the "Wrath of Jonah."

Closing the book, he stepped outside the hut to stretch his muscles, enjoying the rippling strength beneath his skin.

Tomorrow he would search for the caves farther outside the radius where Titus had vanished. Tomorrow he would find him. Another world existed on this island of terrors, and somehow, Jonah knew it was nothing like the ugly world he was forced to survive.

The low growl of a fanged beast drew his attention. He reached for his dagger only to realize he'd carelessly left it inside the hut.

The monster lunged forward.

Jonah managed to sidestep the lumbering beast, but it quickly turned and charged again. He cast an eye toward the hut, calculating. *Could he make it inside without being eaten alive first?*

A piercing whistle cut through the air.

Whimpering, the beast stopped in his tracks, tucked his tail and slinked off into the tangled brush.

Jonah whirled in the direction of the whistle and blew out a long breath. Titus stood a few yards away.

"Hey!" Jonah yelled, scrambling toward the boy. "Please don't run. I need to talk to you."

Titus held a crudely woven basket in his outstretched hands. "Here," he said, shoving the basket into Jonah's arms. "I thought you could use these."

Jonah opened the basket lid and glanced inside. A mouth-watering array of vegetables and fruits lined every corner

"Where did you get these?"

"I grow them." Titus fell in step beside Jonah, heading back in the direction of his hut. "Where I live looks nothing like this." He gestured at the tangled terrain.

Jonah pulled a Mangosteen from the basket and bit into it, ignoring the juice that trickled down his chin. "Take me to your home, Titus," he said between bites.

"I tried to take you, but they wouldn't let me," he replied, stooping to follow Jonah inside the hut.

"Who are they?" Jonah asked, placing the basket on the ground while simultaneously grabbing another piece of fruit. "And thank you for the gift."

"You are welcome. I don't exactly know who "they" are. My father was teaching me about *them* when he disappeared suddenly and never returned. Then, my mother died and that left me ... alone."

Jonah expelled a soft whistle. "Sorry kid. And, sorry I was such a bully the other day. I want to get off this godforsaken island more than anything. I was only thinking of myself."

"Why are you here? Did your mom die, too?" Titus asked innocently.

Jonah leaned back, wishing that was the reason he had been banished here. "I'm here because I was given a choice. I could either go to prison or come here. I chose here. At least I'm not locked in a box, although now I wonder if that would have been easier."

"You must've done something really bad," Titus responded, reaching for Jonah's book, *The Four Agreements*. "My mom used to read me bedtime stories from this book."

"Bedtime stories?" Jonah shoved a hand through his hair. He couldn't bring himself to tell this boy about all the bad deeds that had landed him here. "Tell me more about your mom."

With eyes that widened and glowed an iridescent green at the opportunity to talk about his mom, Titus nodded. "She was beautiful and kind with long, silky, violet hair, and her hands were magical... I mean, she could do such amazing things with them. Both my mom and dad were teaching me the magic, but now, I'm alone and only half-taught." His voice trailed off into a solemn whisper. "I wish my dad would come back."

Jonah's mind scrambled for a logical response to the boy's pain but found none. This kid was obviously the son of a witch and wizard. He recalled stories he'd heard about these people being banished from the mainland hundreds of years ago, and even though Titus appeared to be a young boy of twelve, in truth he could be over a hundred years old.

Jonah prodded. "Tell me about your dad, Titus."

In an instant, the clear blue skies disappeared –

replaced by swirling angry dark clouds, turning day into night. Thunder boomed and lightning crackled in the brush nearby, as a deluge of hard driving rain pounded the hut.

Titus cowered in a far corner. "I don't think I should."

3

*J*onah snatched up his meager possessions as the unexpected deluge continued to pound, unrelenting, upon the crudely made hut.

Water ran in streams, washing away everything in its path. There was no time to waste. He dug the jerky out of the ground and tossed it, along with the books, into a burlap bag.

"Can you make it stop?" he yelled at Titus.

The boy sat dazed, his eyes rolled back in his head, chanting words Jonah could not understand. The fragile walls of the hut began to collapse around them.

Jonah grabbed Titus by the arm, slung the bag over his shoulder and ran. The rain blinded him, as he stumbled over tree roots and briars.

Where could they possibly go?

Titus remained in some sort of a trance, but Jonah pulled him along, the need to protect the kid strong.

Finally, Titus pulled back. He reached into his

pocket and withdrew a large Amethyst Crystal. Placing it on his forehead, he began chanting in a rumbling voice, unlike any Jonah had ever heard.

"Bay of old and sun so bright, clear the mist of clouds at night. I, son of Drake, beseech you; dispel the darkness, bring the light."

Almost as quickly as it started, the pounding rain stopped. The clouds parted, and bright sunshine reflected off remaining droplets on branches and leaves.

"What in the hell just happened?" Jonah asked, shaking water from his hair.

Titus placed the gemstone back in his pocket and shrugged.

Jonah looked at the boy, baffled by his nonchalance. "That's all you've got? A shrug? My hut is destroyed, and you shrug? What am I going to do now?"

"Sorry," said Titus. "Perhaps you shouldn't ask questions about my dad again."

"You can bet on that one," Jonah mumbled, stomping off in the direction of his hut. When he cleared the trees, he gasped.

His hut was intact. Only now, it was larger and sturdier than before, and it even had a door.

Jonah's head swam. *How could this be?* He'd watched it collapse around him. Surely, he was having a wild dream. But this went beyond dreaming. He had to be hallucinating. None of it made sense.

Moving closer to the hut, Jonah spotted a new package sitting near the entrance. For a moment, he stood rooted in the same spot. Titus stood close behind him.

"What? How?" He pointed from the hut to the bag.

Titus shrugged again. "Maybe there is something in it that will answer your questions."

Forcing his feet to step forward, Jonah reached the package and yanked at the tie. He turned the bag upside down and dumped the contents on the hard ground that had been pure mud only minutes before.

Another book and a note fell out. He dropped to his knees. With shaking hands, he unfolded a note and read out loud. "Because you thought of someone other than yourself for the first time in your life."

Titus knelt beside him. "You mean you've never thought about anybody other than yourself your entire life?"

"I suppose not," Jonah muttered.

"But you made sure I was safe, and it seemed to come natural to you."

Jonah reached for the new book. "Dark Side of the Light Chasers," by Debbie Ford. He held it out to Titus. "Ever heard of this one?"

Titus nodded. "It's a workbook of sorts. There are exercises after every chapter."

"Exercises for what?" Jonah thumbed through the pages.

"It's sort of a guided way to work on yourself, to face your shadow self and do shadow work."

Jonah stood. "Shadow work? That makes no sense."

"It will when you read the book. Looks like you have to do some more self-discovery work if you ever want to leave this island."

"I'll read the book alright. I'll learn the right words to say, then I can talk my way out of here."

Titus drew a circle in the dirt. "It doesn't work that way, Jonah. They're not interested in your words. Your actions are what they want to see...And your heart."

Jonah squinted. "How do you know so much about all this, Titus? Did they send you?"

"No. I swear it. I don't know who they are. What I told you is the truth. My father disappeared, then my mother died and I'm all alone on the other side of the island. I would take you there if I could. Then you'd see I speak the truth."

"Okay, kid. I believe you. It's just that you seem to know a lot about all this self-work stuff. More than a kid your age should know."

"It's simple. My mother taught me from these books and many more. She was also teaching me how to grow and use my magic when she died. I have lots of books back at my home. If you want, I could bring you some. Maybe I could even help you learn faster."

Jonah shrugged. "Suit yourself. Bigger men than you have tried," he said, slapping Titus on the back. "Let's look inside my new digs."

With his dagger drawn, Jonah flung open the rickety wooden door to reveal a more spacious and weather-proofed hut. As far as he could tell from the dim light, the inside was empty. The ceiling was now tall enough that he could almost stand upright

He emptied the contents of the bag he'd flung over his shoulder in flight, then tossed the new book into the pile. He quickly dug a hole and re-buried the Jerky.

With some of the vegetables Titus had brought, he could make them a nice soup to eat. He leaned back against the wall and blew out a breath, head spinning with confusion.

He was being forced to take a good, long look at himself, and that frightened him more than anything or anyone he'd ever faced. This was not going to be easy.

If only these challenges required brutal physical strength. That was something with which he was familiar and easily mastered. But, having to look inside himself–well, that might prove a bit more difficult.

4

*T*itus came and went. Jonah never knew when the kid would show up, but when he did, he always came bearing some sort of gift. Jonah now had a more comfortable abode that made daily survival less stressful. And, many days had passed since he'd last seen the fanged beasts. He was sure that was due to the frequent visits from Titus.

He'd scoffed when Titus mentioned that the bigger hut and more comfortable surroundings, allowed him all the time he needed to focus on himself and do the work the Wise Ones were demanding of him.

Nevertheless, within a few days, Jonah finished "The Four Agreements," and started on "The Dark Side of the Light Chasers." He now understood the purpose of the journal.

At the end of Chapter Two, he tackled the exercises.

Question #1: What are you most afraid of?

Jonah thought long and hard as he chewed the end

of his pencil. He didn't have many fears because he'd spent years making sure others feared him. *Okay. Skip that one. Next.*

Question #2: What aspects of my life need transforming?

That answer required no thought at all. He needed to get off this island and back to his turf.

Question #3: What do I want to accomplish by reading this book?

Same answer – to get off this island.

Question #4: What am I most afraid of that someone else will find out about me?

He'd never cared much about what others thought of him. That hadn't been important. *Okay. Skip that one, too. Next.*

Question #5: What am I most afraid of finding out about myself?

He reached for a small mirror Titus had brought on his last visit. His reflection stared back at him. He'd always been told he was handsome with his dark eyes and hair, but that man in the mirror had aged. While he'd worked daily to stay in good physical condition, had he let his mind get soft? Was that what he was afraid to discover? That beneath his hard exterior beat a soft heart? If ever revealed, that bit of information would tarnish his reputation for sure.

He laid the mirror aside and read the next question.

Question #6: What is the biggest lie I've ever told myself?

He knew the answer but refused to write it down. He hated this kind of stuff.

Question #7: What is the biggest lie I've ever told someone else?

The answer to both questions was the same.

He closed his eyes and went back to that dark alley where he'd made his first kill. The scene unfolded in his mind. The look on the boy's face. The begging and pleading. The jeers from others who stood by. A tear squeezed its way out of the corner of his eye and ran down his cheek. He hadn't wanted to do it, but if he'd backed down then, he would've lost their respect. No one had seen him retching behind a trash can a few minutes later, after they'd all moved on down the street. No one had seen him curled up in the fetal position crying, regretting — if only he could take it all back.

He jumped to his feet, stripped naked and dashed straight to the murky water. It didn't matter that gray mud squished between his toes or that the stench of rotted plants attacked his nostrils. A strong urge to wash away that memory was all that mattered. He put his head under and swam back and forth until exhaustion set in, then dragged himself back up on land.

Titus ran to the water's edge to meet him. "Are you okay, Jonah?"

"Go home, kid," Jonah growled.

"Let me help you." Titus placed a hand on Jonah's shoulder.

"I said go home. I don't need any help. I just need to get off this shit hole of an island!" Jonah replied, shoving the boy's hand away, causing his backward stumble.

Titus turned to leave, then stopped. "At this rate,

you'll never get to leave," he said, dropping something at Jonah's feet. "Here … I brought you this."

Dejected, Titus turned and ran away.

Jonah stared at the object, hating himself with every ounce of energy he had for having been so unkind to the boy who had done nothing but help him.

The Wise Ones had been wrong. There was nothing about him that was worth saving.

He grabbed the leather pouch Titus had dropped and pulled the strip that held the pouch closed. Peering inside, a lump filled his throat.

Wasting no time, he ran to his hut, shoved his legs into his pants and set off after Titus. "Hey, Titus. Come back. I'm sorry, kid. I didn't mean to yell at you."

He caught up to the boy when Titus stopped and turned around with a tear-streaked face. "I'm sorry, Jonah. I only wanted to help."

"I know. You don't have anything to apologize for, kid. It's me who owes you an apology. I've been such an ass. I just have so much going on in my head, and all I want to do is go home. It's obvious that ain't gonna happen at the rate I'm going, but this?" Jonah dumped the contents of the pouch into his palm. "What am I supposed to do with these? And what are they?"

Titus shrugged and swiped his nose. "They're sunflower seeds and you plant 'em."

Jonah gestured at the tangled twisted landscape. "Plant them? Where? Look at this place."

"We can clear a spot. It'll just take a little work."

"And this?" Jonah held up a triangular piece of black onyx, outlined in bright red.

"It keeps away bad thoughts."

"Hmm." Jonah studied the shiny black triangle. "Guess I could sure use that." He clapped Titus on the shoulder. "Come back to camp with me and help me figure out a place to plant these seeds." Closing his hand, he funneled them back into the pouch, pulling the string tightly.

Titus wiped his nose again and grinned, falling into step beside Jonah. "Okay. I have lots of them growing on my side of the island. I wish you could see them."

"Me too, kid. Me too."

His mind raced. *Was this all part of his lesson? Instead of fighting the place he'd landed, maybe he needed to help turn it into something more pleasant. Would the simple act of planting Sunflower seeds help?*

He glanced over at Titus. This boy was a mystery. As soon as he thought he had him figured out, he presented something new. What he wouldn't give to see the other side of the island. Titus made it sound like the Land of Milk and Honey.

Once they reached the clearing where Jonah's hut sat in full view, he stopped and scanned the area. "What about over there, Titus?" he asked, pointing to his right. "Would that be a good place to plant?"

Titus quickly studied the spot then shook his head. "Too many rocks. "Maybe up there," he said, nodding in the direction of a hill, sitting behind the hut.

"Whatever you say, kid. Do you have any tools we can use?"

"Yes. I can go get them and come back. That is, if they let me," he added hesitantly.

Jonah's brows furrowed as he paced the area. "I wish we knew who *they* were. I'd sure like to talk to them."

Titus shook his head. "That isn't possible, Jonah. They are everywhere."

"That doesn't make any sense. Are you telling me *they* aren't human?"

"Well, sort of. It's hard to explain." Titus turned to leave. "I'm going to get tools and I hope to be back soon."

"Okay, kid. I'll be here. It's not like I have any other place to go."

As soon as Titus left, Jonah ducked back inside the hut. His gaze landed on the open book and journal. Maybe he'd skip the exercises for now and just read the book straight through. Maybe he'd get to it all later. He flipped the book shut and stacked the journal on top of it.

Jonah stretched out, staring up at the tightly woven grass roof. The memory that had sent him plunging into the water, lingered. He reached into the pouch and pulled out the cool black stone, turning it over between his fingers. Then he spied a small hole at the top of the triangle. He examined the leather string holding the pouch closed. After he unthreaded it, he was not at all surprised to find that it fit perfectly around his neck.

He slid the black onyx onto the leather strip and tied it. *Now, that ought to keep bad thoughts away. But, could it be as simple as that?*

The books he'd been reading talked about shifting

old habits and perspectives and clearing out negative thinking to make room for positive. Next time he'd give it a try. *Cancel, clear, delete,* echoed in his head almost like an outside voice.

5

*J*onah and Titus spent endless hours working to clear the area for planting. He was thankful that Titus was able to make it back with the tools as it made the task easier. Stinging nettles left welts on his skin and a large angry wound covered the back of his right hand where he'd accidentally brushed against one of the deadly, poisonous flowers. Titus had suggested a poultice of mud and herbs for the welts and wounds. Again, the boy's knowledge amazed Jonah. Despite the challenges, they managed to clear a decent sized area.

Titus brought vegetable seeds from his side of the island along with more flower seeds.

It made Jonah happy that Titus spent so much time on his side of the island. Bit-by-bit, Titus brought more of his own things over – so much that Jonah even constructed another smaller hut for the boy.

Shock rippled through him when Jonah realized that

he hadn't cast a glance toward the mainland or scanned the horizon for the rescue boat in weeks.

Slowly but surely, he worked the land while also working on himself.

After hours of digging, hoeing, planting and watering the rows of seeds in the makeshift garden, Jonah stretched out and opened "The Dark Side of the Light Chasers."

Titus dropped down beside him. "Will you read out loud?" he asked.

"Okay. Sure," Jonah replied. "Chapter 6. 'We can now begin to take responsibility for all of who we are, the parts we like and the parts we dislike. At this point, you don't have to like all your aspects; you just have to be willing to acknowledge them to yourself and others. There are three helpful questions you can ask yourself. Have I ever demonstrated that behavior in the past? Am I demonstrating that behavior now? Under different circumstances, would I be capable of demonstrating that behavior? Once you answer yes to any of these questions, you have started the process of owning a trait.'"

"If you ever want to talk about anything, Jonah, I am a good listener."

Jonah stared at him. "Yes, you are. But I don't think I could ever tell you all the things I've done. I don't think you could handle it."

"I know I'm just a kid, but in some ways I'm really not. I experienced a lot with my mom and dad. Stuff that would make your skin crawl. Before we were banished from the mainland, people came in large groups determined to kill our kind. But our magic was stronger than their hatred, so they never succeeded. I've seen my father remove a man's skin without ever physically touching him. I'll never forget the man's screams. I bet you've never seen anything like that, have you?"

"You're right, Titus. I've never seen magic like that. I've only seen the magic I created with my fists, and that was all based out of fear. I had to make people fear me, so they would respect me and leave me alone. I was the king of my turf."

Titus poked at the ground with a stick. "What's the worst thing you've ever done?"

"You're not hearing me. I really don't want to talk about it." Jonah cleared his throat. "I'm beginning to wonder if I really want off this island anymore. Now that you're here, and we're making it better, maybe I don't want to go back to the mainland."

"There's one thing I know, Jonah - we are both being challenged. I can feel my father watching me from somewhere. I feel that he's alive, but I don't know why he doesn't come and get me. Maybe I'm supposed to be here with you."

"If your father is alive and watching, then we need to show him the best of both of us. I've never cared about being the best at anything before except stealing, bullying and even killing. Now I have a strong urge to become something better."

Titus spread his long, webbed fingers out in front of him. "I can't ever go back to the mainland. I would be tortured and probably killed," he said.

"Not as long as I'm alive," Jonah growled.

A long moment of silence passed between them.

"Do you think you could start teaching me your magic, Titus?" Jonah asked.

"I…I don't know," Titus stuttered, his eyes glowing. "I'm not sure it is allowed."

"There's only one way to find out."

"I'm afraid." Titus paced the dirt floor.

"Afraid of what? I'm not going to let anyone hurt you, Titus."

"You don't understand. It's not up to me. And even though you think you can, you cannot protect me. I don't think I'm allowed to teach you the magic."

Jonah stood and laid a hand on Titus' shoulder. "Okay. Don't get all worked up. I'm just trying to understand more."

Titus looked up at him. "It's not that I don't want to. I think you need to learn more about yourself first. If you try to go too fast, you'll burn."

"Burn?" Jonah stepped back. "That's a funny word to use. You don't think your father would skin me alive, do you?"

"I don't know." Titus dropped his hands to his sides. "I can't tell you everything you want to know. You have to find it on your own."

"In the books?"

Titus nodded. "In the books, in your heart, and in your head. When your thoughts become more honest, and your heart more open, you'll find what you seek."

"I suppose that makes sense. You hungry, kid?" Jonah changed the subject.

"Sure. I loved the soup you made yesterday. Can you make it again?"

Jonah laughed and ruffled Titus' hair. "For you, kid, I'll do it. Go gather some firewood."

As the boy traipsed into the thicket, Jonah couldn't help being amazed at how the stinging nettles and venomous flowers always parted to let him through. That was the kind of magic he craved.

Grabbing the pot, he filled it with water and the fresh vegetables Titus had brought, then dug the package of jerky from the ground. Funny that he hadn't realized it before now, but this jerky should have been long gone, and yet every time he opened it, he found several more pieces. He wondered if that was more of the mysterious magic surrounding him.

Titus returned with an arm full of dried wood and Jonah set about building a fire.

A thick silence nestled between them while they ate. Jonah mulled over the words Titus had spoken earlier. He knew beyond any doubt that his thoughts were different than they'd ever been. He'd spent hours reading, reflecting on, and journaling about deep dark secrets that he'd never imagined would see the light of day.

Jonah wanted to purge himself of the darkness he'd embraced for so much of his young life. Shadowed memories of his mother's loving touch came unbidden. He wished he could remember more, but he'd been too young when it all happened. He only knew what he had been told in the orphanage. Someone had killed her. He'd often dreamed of finding that someone and enacting revenge. Now, those thoughts seemed foreign to him, like they had belonged to someone else.

He gathered their cups and strolled toward the water to wash them, but then he froze in his tracks.

6

There it was! A boat sailing straight toward the island. How had he not heard it? His heart thumped. He glanced back at Titus just in time to see him disappear into a thick tangle of brush.

Jonah walked slowly toward the dock as the boat pulled alongside, churning the murky water with its propeller. A rope ladder appeared over the side, and a voice boomed.

"Jonah, you have proven yourself. You are now allowed to return to the mainland. Are you ready?"

He swallowed hard. "I don't know. Can my friend come with me?"

"What friend? We don't see anyone?" the voice replied.

Jonah turned and yelled, "Titus. Titus come back."

He was met with silence.

"Come on, Jonah. Let's go," an impatient voice continued.

"Can I have a little more time to go find my friend?" Jonah asked.

"No. It's now or never. Either go with us or stay here forever. We won't come back." The sound of the engine humming and the blades churning let Jonah know they meant business.

Jonah put one foot on the bottom rung of the rope ladder and began climbing.

"Hurry," the voice ordered.

Now halfway up the ladder, Jonah was still scouring the island as far as he could see, for any sign of the boy.

"Titus!" he yelled again.

All that he could hear was the hum of the boat's engine.

He turned, starting back down the ladder, as the boat began to move away. He jumped the last few feet and landed with a thud on the dock.

Without a backward glance, Jonah ran in the direction he'd seen Titus disappear.

"Titus! Please come back," he yelled at the top of his lungs.

He trampled through the tangled brush, oblivious to the stings against his skin.

Finally, Titus emerged from a strand of trees. "You didn't go."

Breathless, Jonah leaned over and put his hands on his knees, tears streaming down his face. What had he done? He'd given up his only chance to return to the world he knew. When he looked up, he locked eyes with Titus.

"I couldn't leave you here, kid," he choked. "I

wanted to go…I did. But I simply couldn't go off and leave you here alone," he said, dropping to the ground, unable to stand any longer after the hard chase.

"I'm sorry, Jonah. Truly I am, but as I told you, I could not survive on the mainland."

Jonah's chest heaved. Emotion thickened his throat and he swallowed hard. Standing, he turned back toward the hut. "You coming?" he asked Titus.

"I know you think you made a mistake," Titus replied, catching up for the hike back to the hut.

"I don't know what I think. I wanted to go home, but another part of me isn't so sure I can survive on the mainland, either. At least not the way I did before."

When they reached the clearing, Jonah stared at the disappearing boat growing smaller in the distance. He sank down on the sand and let his chin fall to his chest.

Titus dropped down beside him.

A shadow fell across them both, and Jonah jumped to his feet, startled.

Titus looked up and let out a yelp.

A man stood over them wearing a black brocade vest adorned with gold trim, and a red and black silk cape slung carelessly across his shoulders. His polished black boots reached his knees and a large sword hung from his side. Weilderwolves stood like docile pets on either side of the man. Gone were the blood red fangs; they looked up at the man with adoring eyes.

"Father!" Titus scrambled to his feet and ran to the man. "I thought you'd forgotten about me!"

Father and son embraced, then both turned to gaze back on Jonah.

The man's voice thundered, "You did a righteous thing here today, Jonah. You cared more for Titus than you did your freedom." He extended his hand. "I'm Drake."

Jonah swallowed hard, unable to find his tongue to speak.

Titus knelt at his father's feet and kissed his boots.

Jonah wondered if he was expected to do the same. *He certainly didn't want to be skinned alive, so he joined Titus.*

"Up, the both of you," Drake ordered.

In an instant, a woman appeared beside Drake. With long flowing violet hair, dressed in purple, gold and green regality, she resembled a mythical goddess.

Titus flew into her arms. "Mother!" Tears streaked down his face as he choked on his words. "I thought you'd died!"

Jade crooned, "Oh, my son. It was necessary for you to believe you were all alone so that you and Jonah could complete your lessons." She stroked his hair. "I didn't want to leave you, but I believed in you. You were ready for the task, and you did well, Titus, son of Drake and Jade."

Jonah watched with an open mouth. If his life depended on him finding words to speak, he'd surely die this minute.

His gaze returned to Drake. An electrifying aura floated around the giant of a man. It looked much like pictures he'd seen in books of the Aurora Borealis. Jonah sensed the strength of Drake's magic and it ignited a flame inside him. Oh, how he wanted that gift.

But he was a mere mortal. Mere mortals could never possess magic that strong.

His eyes locked with Drake's. Light shot out of them into Jonah's, knocking him backward.

Titus ran to help him up. "Father, Jonah is trapped here. The boat just left."

"I know, son. It was the final test."

Jonah then found his voice. "Test for what, sir? How do you know my name? Are you the one that's been leaving the packages? Did you send the boat?" The questions tumbled out unchecked.

"Come. Sit," Drake said. Red velvet chairs trimmed in gold appeared out of nowhere.

Jonah stumbled forward and found a seat. Confusion filled his head. *Was it possible that he was asleep and dreaming? Had the stress of missing the boat cost him what was left of his sanity?*

He sat and listened.

The Wizard, Drake, spoke with a deep rumble. "You see, Jonah, I knew your mother many years ago. She was a student, learning our ways when the leaders discovered our secret, and killed her." Clearing his throat, he continued. "However, she was more than just a student. She was my lover."

Jonah scooted to the edge of his chair. "You knew my mother?"

Drake nodded. "I have watched and waited to see if you would have the same gift. You've kept it well hidden, but, nevertheless the spark is there."

Jonah waited for him to continue but he didn't. His gaze darted from Drake to Jade, then to Titus. All of this had to be a dream. Nothing about it could be real. And yet, the plush red velvet chair beneath him that had appeared out of nowhere, felt real.

"The gift?" Jonah asked.

"Like I said, your mother, Elizabeth, was my student," Drake went on. "She was learning how to use the magic, and her powers were growing daily. It broke my heart into a million pieces when they killed her." His voice hardened and his eyes flashed. "I wasn't there to protect her, but let me assure you, young Jonah … the man responsible for her death paid dearly."

"Wait," Jonah interrupted. "Let's go back. You said my mother was your lover. Does that mean…?" His words trailed off and he glanced at Jade, too embarrassed to continue.

Drake nodded. "Yes, Jonah. You are my son," he said, reaching for Jade's hand. "It was before I found Jade. I loved Elizabeth, and you were born out of that love."

Again, Jonah's head swam. *The son of a powerful Wizard? How could that be? And yet, it all made sense except for one part.*

He stared hard at Drake. "Why did you let them put me into the orphanage after they killed my mother?"

Drake sighed. "It was a hard choice, but at that time, we were fighting to survive. The leaders were determined to extinguish our kind. Many times, I counselled with the elders. I begged them to let me go for you. But, despite my pleas, they refused. After all, you were half mortal. And, in answer to your questions, yes, I delivered the packages. I brought the boat. I pulled strings to give you a choice between prison and this island. But in the end, the choices were all yours to make."

Jonah ran a hand across his bearded chin. "So, what happens now? Am I destined to exist in this godforsaken place forever?"

"No. But, if you want to learn and grow your magic, you have a lot of work to do."

"Work to do?" Jonah asked.

"Yes. While you are learning of our ways and practicing the magic, you will be given assignments," Drake said. "You see, our original mission on earth was to help mortals find their true selves and lead them into the light and knowledge that lies within each of them."

"How am I going to do that trapped on this island?" Jonah asked.

"I will show you. We will work together." Drake handed Jonah a small staff with a pulsating blue Crystal attached to the end.

Jonah accepted the staff, surprised to feel it vibrating in his hand. "What is this?"

"It is your key to passage through the portal," Drake replied, standing and pointing to the north.

"Portal? I don't understand, sir."

"You remember how you tried to follow Titus the first day you met him, and how the snakes blocked your path while he disappeared through a crevice in stone?"

Jonah nodded.

"This Crystal allows you passage through the portal into our world."

Jonah stared at the glowing gem. "You've been watching us this whole time? I still don't understand."

"It will all become clear." Drake put a hand on Jonah's shoulder. "Gather your things, my son. Let's go."

It only took Jonah a few short minutes to gather his meager possessions. He stuffed everything into the burlap bag and threw it over his shoulder. With a quick backward glance, Jonah bid farewell to the place he'd thought he was doomed to spend the rest of his earthly life. When he stepped away, he watched mesmerized as the hut and everything surrounding it dissipated into a dark vapor. Now, nothing but stinging nettles and tangled brush covered the area.

The four of them, Drake, Jade, Titus and Jonah followed a clear and unobstructed path toward the north.

When they reached the crevice in the rock, Drake stepped aside. "Go ahead, Jonah."

Jonah hesitated. Then, holding the staff in front of him, he cautiously approached the rock. With a swoosh of air, he found himself standing in the most beautiful tropical paradise imaginable.

He turned, to see Drake, Jade and Titus appear in a mist. This was where Titus lived. The enormity of the sacrifice Titus had made to help him, overwhelmed and took his breath away. And, to do it without even knowing Jonah was his half-brother.

He approached Titus with tear-filled eyes. "You gave up all of this to hang out with me in hell?" he asked, gesturing with his right hand.

Titus grinned. "It was better than being here completely alone."

"Thanks, kid," Jonah choked. "I never imagined your world was this."

"And now it's your world, too, Jonah," Titus said gleefully. It was the first time Jonah had seen him smile since their first meeting.

Drake and Jade stood arm-in-arm and observed the two. Jade looked up at her mate. "We did well, my Lord."

Drake lowered his head and claimed her lips. "That we did, my Lady."

"I have but one regret," Jade said. "I wish I had been Jonah's mother."

Drake sighed. "Ah, my love. My life is filled with many regrets, but what happened here today makes up for them all."

7

*J*onah stood frozen in place, taking in his surreal surroundings. Palm trees swayed, turquoise water lapped at the shore, birds chirped, and flowers filled the air with their sweet fragrance. The beauty made his head spin. A large house with stone dragons guarding the entrance, sat approximately one hundred yards away from where he stood.

"You're home, my son. I have dreamed and hoped for this day when I could claim you. You are strong and brave. You're everything my son should be," Drake said, draping his arm around Jonah's shoulders.

"Thank you, sir," Jonah replied, struggling to swallow past the lump that formed in his throat.

"I will teach you our ways and your magic will grow, just as it did with your mother. Of course, you will have to work hard."

"You mean, like chores?" Jonah asked.

A deep rumbling laugh erupted from Drake's chest.

"I guess you could put it that way."

Jade reached for Titus' hand. "Come, my son. We have some catching up to do."

Titus wrapped an arm around his mother's waist, as they walked toward the house, heads together, speaking in low voices. The obvious love between them brought a tear to Jonah's eye. How he wished for the love of a mother, but his mother was dead and not coming back. He was happy for Titus, though. The kid deserved to have his family again.

"I'm ready. What do you have to show me?" Jonah asked, turning to face Drake.

Drake pulled a spyglass from his coat and passed it to Jonah. "Turn around and look through this glass in the direction we came."

Jonah put the spyglass up to his eye and let out a shocked gasp. It was as if none of the rocks or brush had ever existed and he had a clear view of the place he'd just left, less than half an hour ago.

A smaller boat than the one he had refused to leave on earlier, pulled up to the dock and dropped off a passenger. The memory of himself in that exact situation flooded Jonah. But, wait! It wasn't a male. It was a female with long, flaming red hair!

Confused, he turned to Drake. "I don't understand."

"She, like you, has been banished to the island for her crimes. You will be allowed to help her, but only when she is seeking and ready. You can observe her from time-to-time, but you cannot go to her until she does her part of the work."

"So, I will be for her what Titus was for me? Is she

my sister? Is she one of us?" Jonah asked.

Drake chuckled. "No, my son. She is a mere lost mortal, trying to find her way. And, yes, you will help her. As a half-mortal, you are better able to understand and communicate with her. She is your first assignment."

Jonah turned back toward the girl. That unforgettable crushing moment of helplessness, fear and vulnerability he'd first felt when he'd been in her shoes, washed over him. It was almost as if he could read her thoughts and emotions.

Drake laid a hand on his shoulder. "Remember what you've learned. She must seek inside herself for redemption and answers. In the meantime, you will become my student. And, when you are ready, you will meet the others."

"Others?" Jonah stumbled over his words; his thoughts jumbled at the prospect of meeting more like them.

"Yes, Jonah. Others. We are not alone. But, all in good time. For now, let's go to the house and get you a proper bath and some fresh clothes. I have so much to show you, and I've waited so long." He swiped at a tear that escaped.

Jonah nodded, unable to find words. Drake, the powerful Wizard — his father. That realization went beyond his wildest imaginings

In losing everything, Jonah had found all that he sought.

THE END

AUTHOR MESSAGE

And, so it is for us mere mortals from time to time. We often must lose everything to discover our true selves and purpose.

I sincerely hope you've enjoyed Jonah's journey into the depths of hell and onward to redemption. It's been a pleasure to share it with you. My intent is that maybe you'll find bits and pieces of inspiration along the way to do your own shadow work, to face the things that are hidden in the dark recesses of your soul and walk into the magic that exists inside us all.

May your journey bring you to the light and peace your soul craves.

If you are of such a mind to, I'd be honored if you'd leave an honest review!

Jan Sikes

ABOUT THE AUTHOR

I've been an avid reader all my life. I can still remember the excitement that surged through me the first time I realized I could decipher words. Many summers, I won the highest award possible from the Hobbs, NM Public Library for reading the most books.

There's nothing I love more than losing myself in a story.

Oddly enough, I never had any ambition to be a writer. But I wound up in mid-life with a story that begged to be told. Not just any story, but a true story that rivaled any fiction creation. Through fictitious characters, the tale came to life in an intricately woven tale that encompasses four books. Not satisfied to stop with the books, I released music CDs of original music to match the time period of each story segment.

In conclusion, to bring the story full circle, I published a book of poetry and art. I was done.

Wrong!

The story ideas keep coming, and I don't intend to turn off the creative fountain.

I am a member of the Author's Marketing Guild, The Writer's League of Texas, Romance Writers of

America, and the Paranormal Writer's Guild. I am an avid fan of Texas music and grandmother of five beautiful souls. I reside in North Texas.

I'd love to connect! http://www.jansikes.com